Secret Stories from Peachtree Creek
Georgia History (with a Mysterious Twist!)

Marcia Mayo

DEDICATION

This book is dedicated to the second-grade students and teachers at Morris Brandon Elementary School in Atlanta, Georgia.

You taught me so much.

CONTENTS

Acknowledgments   i

1   Frances 2010   1

2   Tuck 1786   8

3   Susannah 1838   22

4   James 1864   41

5   Rosie 1910   56

6   Carl 1964   72

7   Frances 2010   84

8   A Grown-Up's Guide   99

ACKNOWLEDGMENTS

Thanks to Nancy Cardenuto for reminding me to write and to Mary B. Summerlin for reading what I wrote.

Thanks to Karen Evans for letting me read to kids when I was supposed to be administrating.

And thanks always to my kids and grandkids for the best material I could ever wish for

CHAPTER 1

FRANCES
2010

Frances had a secret, and that secret was what she'd just pulled up out of Peachtree Creek, over by the stump her daddy said used to be a giant oak tree, one that was really old, you could tell by the number of rings. The secret was big and heavy and it looked like the flood had uncovered it. Clyde kept getting in the way, running in and out of the creek, spraying water and mud all over her.

Peachtree Creek, which ran through the wooded area behind Frances' house, had flooded for the second time in less than a year, causing all sorts of damage to her home, and all sorts of being mad by her mom and dad. Frances' dad had been laid off from his newspaper job at The Atlanta Journal about eight months before and they were living off her mom's school-teacher salary, which didn't go very far, especially since their house kept getting flooded by Peachtree Creek. At first, her dad had said he was going to enjoy the time and use it to write the book about the '96 Olympics he'd been planning for quite a while, but lately Frances hadn't seen him writing at his computer very often. More often these days, he could be found hitting golf balls from their patio into what he called the "water hazard" that was their back yard. The golf balls all over their yard were also making her mother cranky since she kept talking about the garden they should be digging and the compost bin they should be keeping to save money and the Earth.

"Frankie! You aren't down by the creek are you?" Mom called the day Frances found the secret. As usual, she'd told Frances not to go near the creek, which was stupid. Water moccasins weren't going to show up in their neighborhood just because of a flood and Frances was too smart to step on a snake anyway. Frances's mother called her Frankie because she said she acted more like a Frank than a Frannie, hanging out down by the creek with her dog, Clyde, a rescued critter who looked like a cross between a wolf and a skunk. Frances love that creek. She was always finding the most interesting things down there, things like abandoned birds' nests, dead possums and squirrel skulls. She'd also found some good trash, like an old set of keys attached to a key chain with "Maxine" spelled out in fake diamonds.

Frances knew she would already be in trouble when her mother saw how wet and muddy she and Clyde were so she tried to buy some time. "Hey Mom, I'm just down here in the woods, sitting on our big old stump and reading a book. Clyde's with me." Okay, that was a lie and lying was bad, but this was an important find. Mom, being a teacher, was a sucker for reading, something Frances wasn't all that interested in, along with all the other things her mother wished she would do like take dancing lessons or play the piano. As if she didn't have enough to do, what with going to school every day and having to learn Language Arts and Math and Science and Social Studies and Art and Music and PE. At least having her dad lose his job had made her mom stop talking about

dancing lessons.

"Okay, but don't get dirty and don't go near the creek. That

creek water is filthy. And for goodness sake, don't drink it. And if

you see a snake, walk slowly away from it. Don't try to put it in your

pocket." Mom was obsessed with that snake idea. "And if you see a

hobo, be polite but don't talk to him." It was amazing how long

Mom could holler when she was hollering advice to Frances.

When Mom wasn't busy being obsessed with snakes and

dirty creek water, she worried about the homeless people who

sometimes camped out around Atlanta. For some reason, she

called them hobos instead of homeless people. Frances had never

seen a homeless person or a hobo in her woods, but, like with

snakes, she'd make sure she didn't step on one.

The thing Frances was pulling out of the mud was covered

with some kind of cloth that was hard and crusty and it kept ripping

apart while she pulled on it. And boy, did it stink! Inside was a box.

It was made of metal, maybe tin, and it had the kind of top that pulled off instead of having hinges. It was also really rusty. Frances did wonder if some homeless person had put a snake in there to scare her, but that was a crazy thought, something her mother would think up. She did shake it though to make sure she didn't hear any rattles. Clyde was no help as he nosed the box, just getting in the way.

"Get back, Clyde, you dumb dog." Frances elbowed him to try to get him to move. Frances sometimes called Clyde dumb, which wasn't nice and wasn't even true. He was a really smart dog but sometimes he did get in the way. Like now.

Frances couldn't get the top off. She tried pulling it off. She even got a stick and attempted to pry it off. She turned it upside down and shook it, but still the top wouldn't come off. The box looked old but it was in pretty good shape. It, or whatever was inside of it, was pretty heavy. She needed to find out what was in the box without her parents seeing her. They would just try to take over, maybe make her throw it away. They might even call the police.

"Clyde, it looks like we're going to have figure out how to get this box open without Mom finding out," Frances said as she looked at her dog as if he would offer her some advice, which he didn't.

Frances loved her mother but they didn't see eye to eye about much of anything. To Frances' thinking, her mom would have been happier if Lizzy Sanders had been her daughter.

"Why don't you invite Lizzy for a sleepover? Aren't you friends with her at school?" Mom would say while laying out Frances' clothes each school morning, clothes Frances threw in her closet as soon as her mother walked away. Frances never wore what her mother put out but she kept on putting it out anyway. No, Lizzy was not Frances' friend at school. William Perez was her friend and her mother knew it. She and William had been best friends since they met in kindergarten, back when they'd both wanted to be wrestlers when they grew up.

Frances' dad was more understanding, but that's because he'd really wanted a boy when Frances was born. But now that her dad wasn't working, when he had enough time to do things with her, he just hit golf balls off the back patio. Mom said he was depressed.

So she decided not to tell anyone about the box she'd found, not even William Perez. At least not yet. So she put it next to the old tree stump and covered it with small branches and brush left over from the latest storm, thinking it would be safe unless it flooded again.

CHAPTER 2

TUCK
1786

He was Tucktennagee at his naming ceremony but most people called him Tuck, as if, because he was short and skinny, he couldn't manage and didn't deserve a big name. His mother called him Little Fox, which he didn't mind so much since it seemed to fit. He was small and smart with hair more red than black. He was the youngest in his family and all the other children were girls, girls with long straight black hair like their mother and father. If his parents were sorry that their only son was a small reddish-headed boy, they didn't let on. His home was a happy one, with everyone stretching out on their sleeping mats each night after their evening meal and then greeting the new day each morning as the sun rose overhead giving them their warmth, their food, and their lives.

But Tuck had a secret. In fact, he had a couple of secrets. One secret was his wish that he could go out hunting and trapping with his father and cousins, a wish he couldn't share with his family because they would feel sorry for him and he had too much pride for that. The other secret was what he did when he was down by the creek.

Tuck loved the creek. It had the cleanest, clearest water. It had to be the best drinking water anywhere. He was always finding the most interesting things down there, things like abandoned birds' nests, dead possums, and squirrel skulls. He'd also found other things like old spear points left behind by men who had come that way years before him, and broken cups from other people's dinners long ago. His part of the creek was private, a special place his father had shown him, a place unbothered by women doing their weekly wash or children taking their daily baths.

When Tuck wasn't down by the creek, he liked to sit and listen to the stories his father told around the fire in the evening, stories handed down from long ago about men who had hunted and fished and bravely held off their enemies in the woods around his village, the village known at Standing Peachtree because of the big tree that stood atop a mound of earth nearby. Tuck's village was situated at the intersection of several trails traders used to transport items from near by and far away, things like the cloth his mother used for skirts and scarves, and tools and weapons made from materials the folks in his village couldn't make or grow. The traders, some with skin dark like his but others pale with eyes the color of the sky, also took animal skins, tobacco, and the necklaces his sisters made from bird feathers, seeds, and berries to sell or trade with other men in other places.

Tuck also liked hearing his mother's stories as she worked to grind the corn to make their bread and cut the squash to add to the soup they called sofkee. His mother's stories were funny and sad ones about his own people who had lived their lives on the same land where he now sat and listened, making mind pictures to follow along.

But Tuck's favorite stories were the old ones the village elder told as he tamped down the tobacco in his pipe and then lit it, smoke circling around his turbaned head, stories about the mysteries of the earth and the sun, like the story of the dog that had saved the world from a big flood.

According to the story, a dog warned his master that the earth was going to be destroyed by a flood and he should build a raft. The flood came and the raft saved the man and his dog as they rose above the clouds into a grove of trees. But the man missed his homeland and the dog told him the only way he could go back home would be for the man to throw the dog overboard and into the water. The man didn't want to drown the dog, whom he respected and cared about, but the dog said he was willing to sacrifice his life for the man's happiness.

That particular story made Tuck sad when he thought about it because he loved his black dog, Efv, more than just about anything. Efv was a lucky dog, a three-legged dog, born that way, a dog that should have been left to die as a puppy since he would be of little use in hunting or pulling the sleds that brought back dinner from the forest. But, because he reminded Tuck's family of Tuck himself, they let him live and he became Tuck's best friend and a member of their family. And Tuck knew Efv would sacrifice his life for Tuck's if it ever came to that.

Tuck had not only been born small, one of his legs was shorter than the other, a bent leg that didn't do him much good at all, kind like Efv's missing leg. Tuck got around on a crutch made from a branch of an old maple tree, a beautiful thing his father had created just for him, carved with all sorts of animals, including a red fox on the part where his hand anchored the brace and a three-legged dog that nestled under his arm and next to his heart. Tuck could move pretty fast on that crutch but still his father worried about him, afraid he wouldn't be able to keep up when the men went out hunting for bear, deer, or boar.

But Tuck had another problem. There were some big boys from the far side of the village who came around from time to time, making fun of him and his dog, each of them hopping on one leg while holding on to a tree branch, pretending to be crippled, just being mean. His mother and older sisters all told Tuck to ignore the boys but it made him so mad.

"Gha, Little Fox, you know you are a smarter and better boy than they are," his mother would say, "Just keep on walking. If you don't pay any attention, they will stop."

But Tuck wasn't so sure.

When his cousins were around, the boys never bothered him because his cousins were big and tough and a little bit mean themselves; yet they protected Tuck because he was family. However, Tuck didn't want to complain to his cousins about the boys. He wanted to have the strength, courage, and cunning to defend his own honor.

One thing Tuck could do well with his crippled leg was fish, either with a bone hook on a bit of sinew line or with a knotted net, so he spent a lot of time down by the creek with Efv, whom he lovingly called Slobber for obvious reasons. Tuck caught bluegill and trout while his father and cousins were out hunting and

trapping, and while his mother and sisters were working in the big

garden where they grew most of their food, or cooking their meals

over the hearth that was situated near their home, a good home

built solidly of logs and dried mud.

Tuck's secret by the creek was about the stories he told.

While he was sitting there fishing with Slobber, Tuck would tell

himself stories. Usually he told the stories in his head, but

sometimes, when he was pretty sure no one was around to hear

him, he would tell them out loud and sometimes he would even act

them out, playing all the parts except for the ones he tried to get

Slobber to play. Many of the stories he told were the old ones told

by his father or his mother or the village elder. But sometimes the

stories were new, ones he made up as he went along, stories that

helped him solve problems that were bothering him.

And the problem he was currently trying to solve was the

problem of those big boys and how they were now not only making fun of him, they were also trying to take his crutch away and trip Slobber, making him go nose down in the red-clay dust.

Just recently, while most of the people of the village were enjoying an exciting stickball game, several of the mean boys had caught Tuck and Efv, as Tuck had taken a shortcut behind a small house next to the open field where the game was being played.

"Naken? It's the three-legged dog and the one-legged boy!" the biggest one had taunted. "Let's see how they can walk without their extra legs."

With that, the tallest boy with the squinty eyes grabbed Tuck's crutch and used it to trip poor Efv, who went down yelping. Tuck, tears rolling down his face, crawled over to his dog, who was barking furiously at the boys, and tried in vain to get his crutch back.

Just as the boys were running away holding the crutch in the air like some kind of trophy, the game ended and people could be heard coming their way. As with most bullies, the boys lost their nerve when grown-ups were nearby, dropping the crutch and running off.

The next day, instead of telling his father or his cousins, which would have probably been the best thing to do, Tuck went down to the creek and started a story about solving the problem of the crutch-stealing boys.

"Once there was a small red fox and a dog that drooled a lot," he began. "A pack of big black bears had been coming around trying to scare the fox and the dog."

Slobber watched as Tuck proceeded with his story, looking like he wanted to help but just couldn't quite figure out how.

"Those big smelly bears were tripping up the little fox and the drooly dog," Tuck told as he stood up on his one good leg, hopping over to Slobber and then playfully falling on him until his good sweet dog wriggled to his back so Tuck could scratch his belly.

Suddenly, Tuck stood up again and leaned on Slobber, who had righted himself, grabbing his crutch like a sword, and said loudly, "But then the little fox grew into a great big fox with huge teeth and sharp claws and the dog turned into a giant wolf with fangs and red eyes. The fox grabbed his magic spear and then rode on the wolf's back, knocking down all three of the black bears, putting a spell on them, turning them into scared little rabbits with big ears and fluffy tails. The rabbits turned and hopped away, never bothering the fox and the dog again."

Tuck was happy with his story, so happy that he and Slobber acted it out several times, using the crutch as the magic spear. After a good bit of practice, Tuck could actually ride a short way on Slobber's three-legged back, swinging the crutch at the thorny bushes that grew near the creek.

Tuck never thought his story would come in handy in real life or that he and Slobber would ever be able to truly turn that crutch into a magic spear, but a few days later, the boys came around again. Tuck and Efv were walking back from his aunt's house after delivering a fat trout he'd caught, and just as they were passing through a small wooded area, the three meanest of the boys seemed to appear out of nowhere and surrounded them.

"Grab the crutch," whispered the big one.

"Get the dog," sneered the tall one with the squinty eyes.

The third boy, the one with crooked teeth, moved toward Tuck, ready to push him down and take the thing he needed most to navigate his world, that thing being his crutch. But this time, because of the story, because of all the practicing Tuck and Slobber had done down by the creek, Tuck felt strong and brave, not like a little fox at all but like a big, strong, and very, very mad fox.

"Aaaaaaaaeeeeeeeeeee!!! Eeeeoooooowwww!!!! Yip! Yip! Yip!" Tuck started shrieking and barking like a fox, not being afraid to make a loud noise, understanding that he had every right to make the loudest noise in the world, just like the wild animals did late at night when people were trying to sleep. And Efv took Tuck's lead, remembering his wolf ancestry, snout to sky, howling with all his might and then snapping at the boys with his big, strong teeth.

Tuck did not let go of the crutch when Crooked Teeth grabbed for it. Instead he held tight, climbing on Slobber's back, waving and jabbing the crutch at the boys who stopped what they were trying to do and looked at Tuck, confused and confounded, wondering just what this loud and crazy boy and his dog might do next.

At that moment, a group of women who were down by the creek, doing their wash and gossiping about village news, heard the shrieking, howling, and snapping and came to see what was happening. Even though it appeared that the small crippled boy and his three-legged-dog had things under control, being mothers, they rushed at the bigger boys, yelling for them to stop, grabbing their ears and pulling as they swatted at their rear ends with their wet scrub cloths, taking the boys back to their homes for what was sure to be severe punishment.

Soon, the story spread all around the village, the story of how Little Fox and his drooling dog had made enough noise and created enough confusion, and perhaps even magic, to bring the washing women up from the creek just in time to prevent something terrible from happening.

And so, Tuck's story had come true. He'd become a warrior fox, no longer a little fox, and Slobber had made his wolf ancestors proud, doing what he was born to do. The crutch had turned into a magic spear, holding off the ruffians until the washing mothers could arrive with their loud voices and pinching fingers and swatting hands.

And the bad boys? They'd skittered away like little rabbits, ears appearing to grow longer and longer as the women pulled at them, with the wet whipping cloths looking like they were attaching themselves to their rear ends like little bunny tails.

From that time on, although he was still called Tuck by the people in the village, Little Fox was known as just plain Fox to his family, and he and his crutch and Efv joined his father and cousins whenever they went out to hunt. And whether it was because of the way with which he'd defended himself that one day or because he was growing older, Fox was also given a lot more work to do,

work like hauling wood for the fire or turkeys back from the forest.

But Tuck and Efv still went down to the creek as often as

they could, telling their tales and acting them out, especially the

one about how the fox and the wolf turned bears into rabbits with a

magic spear.

And then one day, Tuck decided to save his story in a special

way. He found just the right stone, long and flat and soft enough

for carving. He used his sharpest bone tool and carved a big fox, a

bigger wolf, and three small rabbits into the stone. When he'd

finished, he took the stone and washed it carefully in the creek and

then he buried it nearby in the shade under a young oak tree, a

small tree hardly more than a sapling.

CHAPTER 3

SUSANNAH
1836

Susannah had been lonely ever since her family had moved

from Virginia a few months before, traveling to the backwoods of

Georgia so her father could open a store in the settlement known

as Standing Peachtree, the ugly store with the horrid Deer Head

nailed to the post near it. She'd had plenty of friends back home in

Virginia and cousins who'd lived nearby, but her family had left

everyone they knew to move to this place with very few people. It

had been terrible and hard and sad.

But then she'd met Senoya. No one had known about

Susannah and Senoya's friendship, no one in Susannah's family, no

one in Senoya's family. That's because Susannah and her family

were white and Senoya and her family were Cherokee.

Susannah couldn't understand why white people and brown people couldn't be friends. Susannah's father called the Cherokee people red Indians, but Senoya wasn't red, she was a pretty brown girl with beautiful black hair, hair so straight it looked like Mama's fancy embroidery thread. Susannah and Senoya had first noticed each other when Senoya's father had brought her into Susannah's father's store to trade tobacco for paper and wool. Although Susannah's father needed the tobacco Senoya's father had and Senoya's father needed the paper and cloth Susannah's father had, they weren't friends. No, not at all. Senoya's father was mad that people like Susannah's father had come and taken over the land that had belonged to his people. Susannah's father was mad because the "red Indians" were causing trouble, some even killing people and burning down houses.

In spite of coming from very different backgrounds, Susannah and Senoya actually lived quite close to each other. Susannah lived with her mother and her father and her grandmother behind her father's store, the store that was becoming known as Buckhead because of the deer head mounted

on the post out front. Everyone in the family worked in the store,

which also included a post office and a tavern. Sometimes men

came into the tavern and drank too much whiskey and they got

loud and mean, so Susannah was only able to work in the store and

the post office, not the tavern. Even though the Cherokee were

allowed to do business in the store, they weren't allowed in the

tavern because Susannah's father said red men couldn't hold their

likker. Susannah thought a lot of white men couldn't hold their

likker either.

Senoya lived down the road from Buckhead. Her house,

which was made of wood and mud, was bigger than Susannah's

house if you didn't count the store and the tavern. Susannah had

never been in Senoya's house because that wasn't allowed.

Susannah and Senoya first become friends when Senoya was

sent to the store to buy a skillet for her mother. Susannah sold her

the skillet and then gave her the wrong change. As Senoya left to walk back home, Susannah ran through the door and out onto the porch with the half penny she still owed her in her hand.

"Wait! Wait! I owe you more money!" Susannah called as she chased Senoya down the red dirt road.

Senoya turned around and looked at Susannah as if she were seeing a ghost. To Senoya, Susannah probably *looked* like a ghost. Her hair was blonde, almost white and her skin was pale, with freckles decorating her nose.

They came face to face, looking like sun and shadow, light and dark. Susannah held out the half penny.

"Here, this is yours. I didn't give you the right change." She paused and then added, "Sorry."

Senoya shifted the skillet and took the coin. "Thank you," she said. After a moment of hesitation, she added, "My name is Senoya."

"I'm Susannah. How old are you?"

"Ten winters. I think you would call me ten years old."

"I'll be ten in September," said Susannah. She thought for a minute, looking at Senoya, and then whispered, "I have a secret place down by the creek. You want to go down there? Nobody knows about it except for me."

Senoya looked at Susannah and said, "I know every place near here. There are no secret places to my people. Which one is it?"

"Over that way," Susannah said as she pointed back behind her father's store. "By the creek. That little cleared-out spot."

Senoya peered at Susannah, her black eyes looking like they were trying to decide. "I have to go home and take my mother her pan. But I think I could meet you this afternoon." She stopped and said, "When the sun is behind the trees."

Susannah looked at the sun and then at the trees and said, "I'll try to get my grandmother to watch the store."

Both girls turned around and headed home, looking back as they walked away, both of them thinking about the secret they just might be sharing, a maybe friendship no one could know about.

As Susannah made her way behind the counter, after passing under the deer head out front, she wondered about Senoya and if she would be able to get away long enough to meet Susannah by the creek.

In spite of hating Georgia and her life there, Susannah loved the creek. It had the cleanest, clearest water. It had to be the best drinking water anywhere. And she was always finding the most interesting things down there, things like abandoned birds' nests, dead possums, and squirrel skulls. She'd even found some old carved stones her father called arrowheads.

Thinking about the creek reminded Susannah that she'd have to ask her grandmother to watch the store so she could escape in order to meet up with Senoya. Susannah's mother and father had taken the wagon down to Terminus to pick up supplies, leaving her grandmother in charge of the store. When Grammy was in charge, that usually meant Susannah had to stay behind the counter, selling thread and bear traps, making change. But Susannah was going to beg her grandmother, saying that she had something important to do. She just hoped Grammy didn't ask her what that important thing was.

All afternoon, Susannah watched the sun, which was taking forever to slide behind the trees. Finally, there it went and Susannah ran into the office in back of the store, where her grandmother was adding up numbers.

"Grammy, can you watch the counter? I need to do something important."

Her grandmother looked up from her work and seemed to be happy to stand up and stretch and do something different for a while. "All right, Honey, but be careful. There's injuns around who are up to no good."

If Grammy had known Susannah was heading out to meet up with one of those "injuns", she would've had a fit. So…..it was a good thing she didn't know.

When Susannah got to her secret place, Senoya was already there, sitting on the bank with her feet in the creek.

Senoya smiled, but then warned, "I don't have much time. I have to get back."

"Me too," said Susannah and she sat down, taking off her shoes, and putting her feet in the creek next to Senoya's feet, sunshine and shadow, cooling themselves in the water.

The next few minutes were spent with each of the girls shyly telling the other a little about her family and her life. To be so different they were very much the same. They each liked certain things about themselves but wanted to change others. They both had chores and lessons and dreams for their future. But they couldn't be serious for too long. Before they knew it, they were splashing each other with creek water and playing a two-girl version of tag between the azalea bushes. Finally, Susannah's mother could be heard calling her, which meant her parents were back from town, so the girls made a pact to try to meet the next afternoon at the same time.

The following day, when Susannah arrived at the creek, Senoya wasn't there, so she sat down and put her feet in the water. She was just sitting there daydreaming, thinking about her secret friend, when she felt a cold nose and a lick on her ear. She jumped up, almost falling backwards, thinking a red fox had sneaked up behind her, but it was just a friendly black dog, one she'd seen before. She was rubbing his silky ears and throwing a stick for him to fetch when Senoya appeared through the trees.

"That's Black Dog. He's been sleeping under our porch and I've been sneaking him scraps," she said. "Etsi says we can't keep him because we have enough mouths to feed. Also, it looks like we will be leaving soon."

"What? Gone? What do you mean?" Susannah asked. "Are you going on a trip? When will you be back?" She was horrified, thinking she would have to go back to just spending time by herself in her secret place, playing by herself, without her new best friend.

"We won't be back. At least not any time soon. Your people have taken our land from us." Senoya hesitated and then added, "Well truthfully, I hear that some of our people just might have sold our land to your people. It looks like we are going to have to leave and go out to where it's cold and dry."

Susannah had heard her father talking about how the red Indians would soon be "gone and good riddance," but she'd never thought how it would affect her. "When will you leave?" She could feel the tears coming to her eyes and she sniffed.

"After a couple more moons. I think *you* call them months," Senoya said, as she took her hand and pressed her heart, looking at the trees and the bushes and the creek as if she were trying to memorize them.

Just then, Black Dog ran up with a stick for the girls to throw and they started playing, running and laughing and just being kids. Susannah put Senoya's bad news in the back of her mind.

Several days later, the friends were sitting side by side next to the creek, wondering what to do. Senoya was trying on Susannah's shoes and Susannah had been attempting to comb Senoya's hair with a pine cone. Suddenly, Susannah had an idea.

"Senoya, do you know how to write?" she asked.

"Yes, some letters. Edoda taught me."

"Who is Edoda?' asked Susannah.

"Edoda is Cherokee for father. Etsi is mother. Although I can speak English, my first language is Cherokee."

"I wish I could speak two languages," said Susannah.

"Maybe I could teach you and you can teach me to write in English."

Susannah grinned and said, "My etsi taught me to write in English and my friend can teach me to write in Cherokee. By the way, what is "friend" in your language?"

"Oginali"

"All right, Oginali. I'll try to bring some scraps of paper and a pencil tomorrow."

"Or we could just write in the dirt with a stick."

Both girls ran off, Senoya to help her mother with their dinner meal and Susannah to take over the counter in the store.

Susannah's father was waiting for her when she walked in the door. He looked mad.

"Where have you been?" he asked sternly. "And what about that creature you've been playing with?

Susannah's heart froze in her chest. Had her father seen Senoya walking into the woods at the same time Susannah disappeared each afternoon? Senoya entered their special place a completely different way, but someone could have seen her.

"What creature?" She was having a hard time looking at her father.

"That black one with the ugly ears and bushy tail. He looks like a mangy wolf."

Susannah was quite relieved, but she needed to think quickly to try to come up with something that would make her father like Black Dog.

"Oh, that's Pat. I named him after Patrick Henry. He's my best friend."

Susannah was telling a lie. Senoya was her best friend, but her father couldn't know about her. Black Dog was her second best friend. On the other hand, Patrick Henry was a famous dead person from Virginia who, for some reason, Susannah's father thought was really great, so she was hoping that, if he thought the dog was named after his hero, he'd allow her to play with him and maybe even keep him..

Susannah's father's face softened as he looked at his daughter. "Well, he doesn't look much like the original Patrick Henry. Old Pat's nose was much longer than new Pat's nose." He chucked and then said, "Maybe it's a good idea to have a dog as a best friend here in the backwoods." He patted the top of her head and continued, "I know this has been hard on you, Susannah, but new families will be moving in as the injuns leave, and one of them will have a little girl your age, someone to be your best friend instead of a dog."

Susannah already had a little girl as a best friend, but she couldn't tell her father that.

A few days later, the girls were practicing their writing lessons in both Cherokee and English. It turned out that the Cherokee alphabet and the English alphabet were more alike than different, although it was easier to spell words with the Cherokee symbols.

Black Dog Pat, their secretly named second best friend who was half white, half Cherokee, all black dog, was trying to catch a fish in the creek by running into the water and diving under, his sharp teeth snapping at the trout swimming by. So far, he'd been unsuccessful.

"I have Black Dog Pat to thank for being able to come down here every afternoon," said Senoya. "Etsi thinks he will save me if something bad happens. That's why she's giving me permission to feed him now. I think she feels sorry for me because we will be leaving soon. Every day when I go home I have to help pack up everything."

"My parents think the same thing about being safe with a dog," said Susannah, refusing to talk or even think about Senoya leaving. "We're feeding him too! No wonder he can't catch a fish. He thinks his food should come in a bowl now."

Senoya added, "And I think he's getting fat!" She stopped and looked at Susannah. "Susannah, Etsi told me we can't take a dog with us. Will your parents let you keep Black Dog Pat?" Her lip quivered but no tears were allowed to leave her dark eyes.

Susannah looked at Senoya, wondering if her heart was going to break in two. "Yes. I'll take good care of Pat and I'll think of you every time I look at him." She looked the other way as she wiped her face with her skirt.

For the next month or so, as spring moved toward summer, Susannah, Senoya, and Black Dog Pat met secretly almost every afternoon. On one of those afternoons, Susannah brought a small book to the creek, a journal her mother had given her for her ninth birthday, a place for her to practice her writing.

When Senoya arrived, Susannah was writing in the book using a pen and ink. Senoya had seen books before and had watched her father using a pen when he was working in his ledger, but she'd never known there was a kind of book for just for a girl to write in.

"Oh!" She said. "What is that?"

"It's a place for us to write our story," answered Susannah. "We can write about how we met and our secret place."

"And we can write it in both of our languages," added Senoya.

The girls took turns making letters and words and drawing pictures in the small journal, dipping the nib of the pen in the ink, trying to keep from making drips but then laughing when they did. Black Dog Pat was generally getting in the way, so they shooed him when he stuck his nose in their business, telling him to go play somewhere else.

When they'd worked for a few minutes, Susannah looked at Senoya and carefully asked, "Senoya, will you miss me when you leave?"

"Yes, my olginali, I will miss you very much." Senoya, who never cried, had tears welling from her black eyes. "I will miss my home and my people's land most, but I will also miss my dog and my best friend."

They sat and looked at each other for a minute, then dried their tears with embarrassed giggles, and got back to work.

After they had written an entire page, Susannah said, "Now, we've got to figure out where to keep it. I can't take it home where my mother might find it."

"What if we dig a hole and bury it so it will be safe but we can still find it?" asked Senoya.

"But it will get dirty."

Senoya thought for a minute and then said, "I've got an old scarf at home. I tore it on a nail and I've been afraid to tell Etsi. I'll go get it. We can wrap the book in it."

"And I can get a wooden box from the store. There are some out back. I think I saw one big enough but not too big."

Both girls took off for home and were able to keep from running into anyone who would ask why they needed a torn scarf or a box from behind the store. When they returned, they started looking for just the right location, discussing the merits of this place or that. However, Black Dog Pat made the decision for them when he started digging a hole in the shade under an oak tree near the creek.

When they walked over to check their dog's progress, they found a smooth stone in the bit of dug-up red dirt that wasn't already on his nose.

It was only after they washed the stone in the creek that they noticed the carvings.

CHAPTER 4

JAMES
1864

James sat up after drinking, having cupped his hands for a big old mouthful of delicious creek water. This creek had to have the cleanest, clearest water, the best drinking water anywhere, much better than that musty smelling water back home.

James and his father had been hiding out for a few days, waiting, and he'd found the most interesting things down by the creek, things like abandoned birds' nests, dead possums, and squirrel skulls. He'd even found what looked to be an old beer bottle.

James was a talented kid. He had a beautiful singing voice and a good story-telling voice. Since he and his father had left their home in South Georgia, they'd had to be careful, traveling and making up reasons why they were on the road. Even though they were supposed to be free, they weren't free to join the Union Army, which is what his daddy wanted.

That's the secret that James and his daddy shared. If people found out they were looking to join the Union Army, they could be arrested and put in a Confederate prison, like the one down at Andersonville, and they'd heard that *nobody* wanted to end up at Andersonville.

James had been born in South Georgia on a medium-sized cotton plantation. His mother had died trying to have him so he didn't remember her at all. For his whole life, it had just been his daddy and him, along with the other slaves who lived and worked on the plantation. They'd all stayed in small cabins on plantation property, homes owned by their masters, along with everything else. James' daddy had told him about his mama, about how his mama and daddy had met and fallen in love and, since slaves weren't allow to get married, how they'd had their secret ceremony, jumping the broom, with their friends watching and celebrating.

A couple of years before, at soon as they'd heard about emancipation, most folks thought they'd be free, which they were supposed to be, but their masters had taken their sweet time letting them know. Plus, where could they go? What could they do? They didn't have any money and people weren't interested in hiring them. So James and his daddy had stayed on the plantation for a while, doing their same jobs, expecting the owner to pay them at some point, which he never did.

Finally, when his daddy had heard the Union Army was heading to Georgia, the army that was going to make sure they stayed free, he'd decided he and James should leave in the middle of the night and start walking north, hitching rides when they could, maybe even riding the rail from Macon to Atlanta, to try to meet the Union soldiers along the way. His daddy had picked up some farm jobs from people who usually just paid with a place in the barn to sleep and some food. James, on the other hand, had been paid in real coins on the side of the road when he would tell a funny story or sing a good old church song. People seemed to like it when he played the little flute his daddy had made for him, the flute his father had learned to carve from an old Indian who lived out in the woods down in South Georgia. That flute was the only possession James had brought with him other than the clothes on his back. He didn't even have shoes. It was a good thing it was summer.

Although they had to be careful since lots of people thought they should still be slaves, James and his daddy would stop in a small town and James would start blowing a tune on his flute and pretty soon he'd be singing in that beautiful voice he had, the voice Daddy said he'd inherited from his mother. He'd sing a church song like Swing Low Sweet Chariot. White people just loved to hear black people singing church songs. What those white people didn't know was that many of the songs black people sang had more to do with freedom than with church.

One of James' favorite songs to sing was Wade in the Water, which went something like this:

Wade in the water,
Wade in the water children.
Wade in the water
God's gonna trouble the water

Who's all those children all dressed in Red?
God's gonna trouble the water.
Must be the ones that Moses led.
God's gonna trouble the water.

What are those children all dressed in White?
God's gonna trouble the water.
Must be the ones of the Israelites.
God's gonna trouble the water.

Who are these children all dressed in Blue?
God's gonna trouble the water.
Must be the ones that made it through.
God's gonna trouble the water.

White folks thought the song was about God and Moses, but it was really about the Underground Railroad, which was a secret route for slaves to take in order to reach freedom up north or even in a place called Canada. James' favorite line: *God's gonna trouble the water* meant that, by going into rivers with a strong current, the dogs and men who were after them would lose their trail.

Somehow, after lots of miles walking, and some miles riding in the back of wagons or hidden in a freight car, often laying low during daylight hours, James and his father had ended up on the edge of Peachtree Creek, just north of Atlanta. They'd been hiding out for a couple of days in a cleared out area, a place with a great big oak tree and some pretty azalea bushes and they'd tried to make it feel like home. It was hard not having a home, even if the only home they'd ever had wasn't really their home at all.

James and his daddy had heard that Peachtree Creek was where the Union forces were heading and they'd also heard that the Confederates were going to hold them off somewhere nearby. It was mid July and hot, but the creek was cool what with the big trees that surrounded it. Someone had told Daddy that the Union Army was headed south, led by a general named Sherman. Daddy wanted to join the Union Army and he wanted James to be a water boy. James was too young to be a soldier but soldiers in battle needed people to bring them water and James was old enough to do that.

James was scared. He'd never been in a war before. They hardest thing he'd ever had to do was to pick cotton all day in the hot sun. Picking cotton was hard work, but it wasn't scary, unless you stepped on a rattlesnake. He didn't quite know what soldiers did in a war, but he knew that lots of Confederate soldiers had died. Maybe the Union soldiers had had better luck.

James was a singer and a story teller, not a soldier. Not even a water boy.

Suddenly, while James was sitting by the creek and worrying, wondering where his daddy had got off to, a black dog ran up to him. James jumped up and started climbing up the big old tree, thinking the Rebel Soldiers or his former owners were after him, sending in a black dog to sniff him out. But after a couple of minutes of sitting in that tree watching that dog watch him, wagging his tail and grinning, slobber drooling down his cheek, James decided the dog must be friendly, so he climbed down and gave him a pat on the head.

"What you doing here, boy?" he asked. "Don't you know there's going to be a war? It's gonna to be dangerous for both a boy *and* a dog."

James thought that this black dog might not understand any of his jokes so he decided to sing him a song, tuning it up with his flute. He would have to sing quietly to make sure nobody heard him, nobody other than this dog and his daddy who was probably out trying to find out what was what.

James sang another secret song:

Steal away, steal away!
Steal away to Jesus!
Steal away, steal away home!
I ain't got long to stay here!

"Who you singing to?" James' daddy asked as he came through the trees with what looked like it just might be supper under his arm.

"This is Billy. I named him after General William Tecumseh Sherman, who's headed this way," said James as Billy, the dog, not the general, looked at them and smiled.

"Well, I'm sure the general would appreciate your thoughtfulness in naming a mongrel dog after him, but you know we can't keep him. We can barely feed ourselves."

"I know, Daddy. Do you think I could keep him just this one night?"

James' father looked at him and then at Billy and said, "I guess we got enough hard tack and salt pork to share for one night."

"What's hard tack? That don't sound good," observed James, looking at what his father had under his arm.

"From what I hear, it ain't good. But if we're goin' to be soldiers for General Sherman, we got to learn to eat like them. I ran into a couple of Union soldiers about a mile from here. They were good enough to share some of their food with us and they told me

49

to expect something big to happen some time around tomorrow or so."

"I guess that's good news," said James, who was more interested in seeing the hard tack than thinking about anything exciting that might be happening. They hadn't eaten at all that day. "Now, where's that hard stuff?"

James' father showed him what was under his arm, starting with the salt pork, which James recognized, as he'd been eating it his entire life. The other thing looked like a big square biscuit. James took it and tried to bite into it.

"Ow, that just about broke my tooth," said James. He held it out for Billy to sniff. Billy sniffed but didn't try to take it from James. He did look with interest at the salt pork though, wagging his tail.

"Yeah, they said we'd need to hit it with something or soak it in order to eat it. Since we don't have anything to hit it with except your flute, I think we better dip it in the creek. At least it ain't wormy. The soldiers I talked to said hard tack sometimes gets so

wormy they call the chunks of it worm castles because of the

maggots climbing in and out."

James thought it was no wonder Billy wasn't interested in hard

tack, and since he wasn't going to chance breaking his flute by

hitting the big old biscuit with it, he walked over to the creek and

dipped it in. One dip didn't seem to do the trick, so he dipped it

again.

A while later, after James, his daddy, and Billy had tried to eat

the tough salt pork and the even tougher hard tack, they decided to

celebrate with some blackberries they found by the creek and a

sweet song sung by James.

He sang his favorite, which started with:

Amazing Grace, how sweet the sound,
That saved a wretch like me....
I once was lost but now am found,
Was blind, but now, I see.

When he got to the third verse, it made him think about what might

happen the next day.

Through many dangers, toils and snares...
we have already come.
T'was Grace that brought us safe thus far...
and Grace will lead us home.

After he finished, James asked his father, "Daddy, do you think there'll be a battle here tomorrow?"

James' father was lying back, resting as evening cooled the air. He said, "I don't know James, but expect there will be. Both sides seem to be itching to fight."

James asked, "Daddy, is right to be scared?"

"It's not only right. It shows good sense. But James, they ain't gonna let either of us fight. You're too young and I ain't trained. I found out today you got to be trained to be a soldier. So, we're just going to be there to help out. Do what needs to be done. Bring 'em water or a rag to wipe their faces." James' father looked at his son, his only child, and added, "You know I love you too much to put you in harm's way, but what we're doing here is important. We got to do our part for our future. I want you to be able to do whatever you want in this world. You might even have the chance to learn to read and write. I'm laying all my hopes on you, James."

James suddenly felt brave and proud. And he was excited to think that he might some day have the opportunity to learn how to read. On the plantation where he'd been born and raised, slaves hadn't been allowed to do any book learning, but, even if they'd been allowed, there'd been no one to teach them, at least no one interested in taking the time.

That night, James couldn't sleep. Billy kept getting up off the ground, then licking himself and shaking off. A couple of times, he cold-nosed James as James lay there in the grass and leaves. Finally, James got up quietly and headed toward the creek, Billy by his side. James was worried about his flute. It was the only valuable thing he had, valuable because his father had carved it and also valuable because it helped James to sing his songs, the songs that told the secret stories of his people. He wanted to find a place to hide it before the battle started. He didn't want to take the chance of losing it or having it get broken or shot up. It needed to be a good hiding place, but one where he could find it again.

Billy seemed to know what James was doing, what he was looking for. He started nosing around under a huge oak tree, scratching around in the red dirt, the full moon showing him the way. James thought Billy had the right idea. He could hide the flute in the dirt under the big oak tree. It was the biggest tree in the grove of trees next to the creek. He'd definitely be able to find it after all of the excitement was over. That's if he lived long enough.

As Billy was digging with his big feet and strong snout, James noticed what looked to be a wooden box. After he pulled it up out of the dirt, he opened it and found a carved stone and a book wrapped in some kind of cloth. When he looked in the book, it made him even more excited to believe that, one day, he'd learn how to read. That way, he'd know what those marks were all about.

James decided to keep his discovery secret. He'd tell his Daddy after they did their part for the Union Army. He placed his flute inside the box with the stone and the book and covered it up again.

Two days later, Peachtree Creek no longer had clean, clear, good-tasting water. Filled with the aftermath of war, it ran red with blood, and bullet shells and abandoned tin cups littered the stream.

CHAPTER 5

ROSIE
1910

Rosie coughed as she ripped out a seam. In spite of the big house having gas lights, it was dark in the small room she shared with Belle. Although Rosie was grateful that the rich Atlanta folks were giving them a place to stay while her aunt made the beautiful white gown and big trousseau for their daughter's fancy wedding, she had a sad secret. Rosie's secret was that she was homesick.

Rosie's Aunt Belle was one of the best seamstresses in Atlanta, so good that ladies had her come live with them while she sewed their dresses. She was especially known for her trousseaus, which were all the clothes a bride needed for her wedding and her honeymoon. Rosie hadn't even known what a trousseau was until

Aunt Belle had told her.

Until just a month ago, Rosie had lived with her mother and her

big brothers at Whittier Mill up by the Chattahoochee River.

Everyone in her family worked in the mill, including Rosie, even

though she was only ten years old. She had started out as a bobbin

girl but had moved up to spinner, making seven dollars a week. But

then the coughing had started. At first, her mama had thought it

was just a cold or the spring flowers that were causing her cough,

but it got worse and worse. Mama finally took her to the mill

doctor who said she might have brown lung from breathing in all

the cotton lint in the spinning room and, if she didn't have a break,

she could die.

Rosie didn't want brown lung and she didn't want to die, but

Mama couldn't afford to feed her if she didn't work. So Mama had

written Aunt Belle a letter, asking her if Rosie could live with her for

the summer, maybe learning to sew and helping out with her

trousseau-making, and maybe getting out into the summer sunshine some. Aunt Belle was Mama's sister and so she said yes.

It was exciting riding the electric street car all the way from Whittier Mill to West Paces Ferry Road, but life in the big old snooty rich Atlanta house was kind of boring. Rosie didn't have any friends and she had to be careful not to break anything. There were fancy vases and breakable doodads all over the place in that big old house.

Although Belle said she liked Rosie's company and that she was a big help with the sewing, Rosie knew it was hard on Belle. They had to share a bed in a tiny hot room up in the attic and sometimes Rosie's hands weren't as clean as they should be while she was working with the cloth. And then there was the cough that kept them both awake at night.

Sometimes Belle told Rosie to run outside and play, to get some fresh air for her cough. The rich folks had a huge estate with a yard so big it backed up to Peachtree Creek, which Belle said was a tributary off the Chattahoochee River. Knowing this made Rosie love the creek, because it made her feel like it was a connection to home. Sometimes, she would pretend she could swim from where she was staying in the rich part of Atlanta known as Buckhead all the way to the poor part where she lived with her mother and her brothers. Although some people said that trash from Whittier Mill was making the Chattahoochee so dirty the water wasn't much good any more, Rosie thought the water from the Chattahoochee was the best water in the whole wide world. And because Peachtree Creek water was the exact same water, it was good too.

Rosie had found the most interesting things down by Peachtree Creek, things like abandoned birds' nests, dead possums, and squirrel skulls. She'd even found an old tin cup that looked like a bullet had been shot through it. Aunt Belle had said finding the tin cup with a bullet hole in it made sense because that area of Atlanta had been where a big Civil War battle had been fought about fifty years earlier, a battle known as the Battle of Peachtree Creek. The thought of having soldiers fight right where she was living made Rosie shiver like a cold wind had come through, even though it was hot as blazes everywhere.

One afternoon, Rosie ran out the back door of the big house and down to the creek. She couldn't contain her excitement. She had a letter! An actual letter addressed to *Miss Rosie Grace McGee,* in care of her Aunt Belle, right on the street where she was staying for the summer. It even had a two-cent stamp glued to the envelope.

Rosie recognized the penmanship: the curly *a* and the very straight *i.* She knew it was from her best friend, Sarah Jane Jackson. Sarah and Rosie worked side by side at the mill six days a week from seven in the morning until four in the afternoon, spinning and untangling the yarn, climbing up and down on the machines to make sure the cotton was attached correctly and not clogging the gears. And then, after work three days a week, they would run over to the settlement house where, from 4:30 to 7:30, Miss Jenkins taught them to read and write and do their sums.

Rosie loved school and missed it when it closed down for the summer. She loved hearing the stories Miss Jenkins read to them and the stories she was learning to read for herself. In fact, Rosie loved mill life. Even though it was hard to work such long hours, inside a hot room every day spinning the yarn that was used to make cloth that was then used to sew socks and gloves and sometimes even fire hoses, there were lots of fun things to do at Whittier Mill, things like skipping with Sarah to the company store for penny candy (when they had a penny) and sitting in the grass listening to the music from the brass band in the bandstand on Parrott Avenue. Sometimes, they even had picnics in the park.

Rosie sat by the creek, her feet dancing around in the cool water. Although looking at the envelope and seeing Sarah's writing made her happy, it also made her feel a little like crying. She held the letter to her chest, getting up the nerve to open it. She hoped it wasn't bad news. Rosie knew that finding the money for a sheet of paper and an envelope plus more money for a stamp would be hard for Sarah. She pulled on the flap, tearing it a little.

Dear Rosie,

I hope you are not too sick any more. I miss you every day. The other night my sister, Kate, and me sat under the stars to listen to the band. I saw your brothers, Frank and John. They was horsing around with some other big boys and they got in a fight. I think they got took to the jailhouse. But they are out now because I saw them at the mill yesterday. Please come home soon. It's no fun at all here without you.

Your friend, Sarah.

Rosie read the letter three whole times. She thought Sarah had done a good job of making her words, and her spacing was just about perfect. She began to think she needed to write back to Sarah and tell her about living in the big house and about the beautiful wedding dress Belle was sewing, about the beads and the lace and the yards and yards of white cloth, cloth white as snow, so different from the cloth they made at the mill.

But Rosie didn't have any paper to write on. She guessed the rich people probably had some, but she was pretty sure they wouldn't want her to use any of it. And where would she get a pencil and an envelope and a stamp? She didn't want to bother Belle, who was working so hard.

As Rosie was sitting and thinking and worrying about how she could write a letter back to her best friend, Sarah, loneliness washed all over her like a flood. Tears came to her eyes and her nose started running. This led to sniffing and snuffling, which she was doing a good job at when she heard another sound coming from under an azalea bush behind the huge old oak tree next to the creek.

At first Rosie thought a bear might be behind the tree, even though she was sure the rich folks didn't allow bears in their big old yard. But the noises sounded like little baby noises, so she got up the nerve to go look and what she found was a black mama dog with three little puppies. They were hidden under a big azalea bush and when Rosie peeked through, the mama dog looked worried, but what could she do with her three babies in the middle of their dinner?

After what seemed like a long time of Rosie sitting and waiting, trying not to make too much noise in her excitement, the mama dog came out from under the bush and sniffed her all over. Rosie must have passed the sniff test because the mama dog licked her face and hands and then went back to her babies.

So now Rosie had another secret and she had four friends, the mama dog and her three puppies. She also had a reason to be happy staying at the big old rich people's house that summer and she didn't feel quite as homesick any more. Soon she was saving part of every meal to give to the mama dog so she could make milk to feed her babies. She also named them after the people in her family, which made sense because the dogs all had curly black hair just like Rosie even though they didn't have her blue eyes. The mama she named Sally after her own mother, and the puppies were Frank and John and Belle, since she didn't think it was right to name a puppy after herself.

Sally seemed to know she wasn't allowed up close to the house, but the babies were bad and Sally and Rosie were always having to go get them and take them back to their azalea bush home. Because of Sally and her babies, Rosie was spending more time down by the creek and less time helping Belle, but Belle didn't seem to mind and Rosie's cough had mostly gone away what with all the sunny days she was spending out in the fresh air.

One afternoon a few weeks later, Sally was digging a hole next to the old oak tree, trying to bury an especially delicious soup bone Rosie had managed to get from the back porch where the cook had put it out with the other garbage, when she unearthed what appeared to be a wooden box. When Rosie first saw it, she wondered if wooden boxes down by the creek were where rich people kept their money and if she was getting ready to get herself and her Aunt Belle into big trouble. But the box looked old and crusty and it was falling apart and Rosie figured rich people didn't let their money boxes get old and crusty.

"Move, Sally!" Rosie said as shooed Sally out of the way and pulled the box out of the ground. She managed to get it open, marveling at what she found.

One of the things in the box was a book. Rosie opened it up and saw writing. Some of the writing made sense and some didn't. It looked like the book had gotten wet so a good many of the pages were ruined and stuck together, but she could still read a little of what was in it.

Rosie closed the book and put it back with the other things in the box. She needed to think about her discovery and decide if she should tell Aunt Belle.

A few minutes later, as Rosie was lost in thought about what she'd found, Sally and her puppies sitting in the sun beside her, she heard what sounded like a footstep behind her, someone stepping on a twig.

Before she could turn around, she heard a woman's voice, sounding stern, "What are you doing and where did these dogs come from?"

Rosie's heart lurched as she looked back, feeling surprised and caught and guilty of all sorts of things; things like feeding a stray dog and her puppies with stolen scraps of food and not telling about a treasure in the back yard behind rich people's big old house. She jumped up, trying to brush away the leaves from her dress, feeling embarrassed by her dirty bare feet. She realized that the young woman looking at her with a frown was Mr. Morrison's daughter, the soon-to-be bride who was the reason for Aunt Belle's job and for Rosie even being in the yard.

Rosie had seen the bride going in an out of her dressing room, handing Belle parts of dresses, a crinoline here or an embroidered collar there, but she'd never spoken to her before. She was scared, certain she was going to be the cause of Belle losing her job and Mama being upset and mad because Rosie would have to return home early before her lungs were ready to go back to work.

"Uh, I was just down here playing; I'm so sorry. I'll clean up this mess, but please don't let anyone hurt the puppies or their mama. They didn't do anything wrong. This is all my fault." Rosie could understand Mr. Morrison sending Belle and her packing, but the notion of his running down to the creek with the gun she assumed he had locked away somewhere in his big old house, and then shooting at Sally and her babies was so horrible, she was prepared to defend them with her own life.

At that, the woman's face softened and she said, "Oh no! I'd never hurt a dog." Then she looked at Sally and continued, "This mama reminds me of the dog I had when I was a little girl. Her name was Daisy and I loved her more than just about anything."

As Rosie watched with unbelieving eyes, the grown woman who was soon to be a wife had collapsed into the leaves and pulled off her own shoes and was cuddling Sally's babies in her lap, giggling as they licked her nose and talking about how precious they were.

Then the woman asked, "What are their names?" She asked the question in such a way as to let Rosie know it was all right for her to be down there by Peachtree Creek with dogs she'd known long enough and well enough to name.

Before long, Rosie had learned the bride's own name was Louisa and Louisa had played down by the creek when she was a little girl, playing with Daisy around the very same bushes Sally had chosen to have her babies.

But Louisa had never seen the box before, and she was surprised that Sally had uncovered it in the same place she'd played as a child. At first, Rosie thought Louisa would act all grown up, wanting to report the box to her father or maybe to the police, but she didn't. Louisa said she thought the unusual markings in the book were something an Indian might have written, which made Rosie nervous because she'd heard about wild Indians and how they'd once lived in Georgia.

Before Rosie knew it, Louisa and she had become good friends, and Louisa had even offered Rosie her pen and some of her very own stationary to use to write Sarah back. And Louisa had also come up with the idea of adding something to the box and re-burying it.

Several weeks later, Rosie was on the trolley again, heading back to Whittier Mill and to her mamma and her brothers and her best friend, Sarah. She was glad to be going home but she would miss Belle and Louisa, and of course, Sally and her puppies. But her summer had been a good one. Belle had finished Louisa's trousseau, and Belle and Rosie had even been able to attend the wedding, sitting on the back row of the big church with the other help. Mr. Morrison had surprisingly taken a liking to Sally and her babies after Louisa introduced them, saying that he needed some new life in the big old house, since his baby girl had gone and gotten married and left him.

Rosie just hoped her secret would be safe in the ground. Louisa had promised, and Sally certainly wasn't going to tell, but no one knew what might happen if she ended up with a juicy bone to

bury.

CHAPTER 6

CARL
1964

Carl was tired of handing his daddy nails and finding the

hammer. He was also tired of cleaning up after the men finished

for the day, picking up trash and left-over pieces of lumber. He

worked hard at getting it all up, so that none of the trash ended up

down by the creek. Carl thought the creek was beautiful, but

sometimes he found paper cups, cigarette butts, or Coke cans

floating in it, which made him mad.

It was hot and Carl wanted to go home to supper. He wasn't

sure this was how he wanted to spend his summer vacation. At first

the idea had sounded good, helping his father at the construction

site and not having to stay with Grandma and his little sister, watching Grandma's TV shows all day, while his mother was at work.

"Hey Pops, I'm going down to the creek to wash my hands before we go home," said Carl. This was sort of true, but mainly Carl wanted to go sit under the big old oak tree that was going to be cut down in a few days, taken down because its branches were too big and old fashioned to fit into the plan for the five modern houses that were going to be built on property that had once been a big estate up in the north part of the city where the rich white people lived.

Carl sat in the shade of the tree, looking up at a bird's nest, hoping the baby birds had already flown away since their home was getting ready to be destroyed when the tree was cut down. Carl was a dreamer, something that annoyed his parents, who wanted him to be more of a doer.

"Carl," his father would say, "Get off the couch and let's go shoot some hoops." Carl would get up and go outside with his dad and try to get the ball into the net that was attached to the side of their house. He did this without much optimism or success.

"Carl," his mother would say. "Put that book away and come help me in the kitchen. This supper isn't going to put itself on the table." Carl would close his book, push his glasses up on his nose, and wander in to help put out the silverware.

"Mama, do you think Dr. King had to help out with supper when he was a kid?" Carl might ask, offering a question that would usually get a smile from his mother. Carl's mother loved Dr. Martin Luther King, who was from their hometown of Atlanta, Georgia.

"I expect he did," Mama would answer. "That's why he turned out to be such a good and smart man."

Sitting under the big old, soon-to-be-gone tree, Carl thought about the past year. It had been a very good year and a very bad year. Martin Luther King had led his march on Washington and given his "I have a dream" speech, which was good. But then President Kennedy had been killed, which was terrible. And, just a few days ago, the Civil Rights Act had passed, which was terrific.

The Civil Rights Act said that all people, black and white, had the

right to do the same things, things like going to the same school and

shopping at the same stores and sitting wherever they wanted on a

bus.

But Carl was a little bit scared. Although he was excited about

all the rights he and his family and friends would have, he didn't

really know any white people. He'd seen them on the street and his

daddy's big boss was white, but he'd only met him once when he

came to check on the crew to make sure they were doing things

right. His mother worked with some white ladies but he'd never

been to his mama's job. At school all his teachers were black just

like him, and all his friends were some color from dark black to light

brown, but nobody white. His neighborhood was all black and so

was his church.

Was somebody going to make Carl go to another school, a

school with kids and teachers he didn't know? A school far away

from home? He knew that some of the high schools in Atlanta had black and white kids going to them, and he'd seen the news on TV with black children being led by white policemen into a white school with white people yelling at them and throwing things. Carl was all for civil rights and freedom, but he didn't know any white people and he didn't want to go to another school. And he definitely didn't want people throwing things at him.

And then there was Ernest, who was Carl's best friend. Carl and Ernest had gone to school together since first grade. They would meet every day during recess to talk about The Amazing Spider Man and Batman and Robin and all the other heroes they read about in their Marvel and DC comic books.

"I got my allowance and bought the new Aquaman. Do you want to read it?" Ernest might ask when they met by the fence. "Heck yeah," Carl would answer, and, pretty soon, Arithmetic and Spelling would be forgotten as they read and talked about the latest adventures of their favorite characters. Sometimes they would work on their own comic books, the ones they were writing and illustrating. Both wanted to be comic book writers when they grew up, something Carl couldn't tell his parents since they wanted him to go to Morehouse College like Dr. King, and Carl was pretty sure he couldn't learn to be a comic book writer at Morehouse.

As Carl was sitting under the oak tree and thinking and wondering if Dr. King had read comic books when he was a kid and what he would have done if he'd been forced to change schools, a black dog ran up to him. Carl loved dogs and wanted one, but his dad said they had enough mouths to feed without feeding the mouth of a dog. The dog had what looked to be a dead possum in his mouth and he offered it to Carl.

Carl jumped up and hollered when he saw the smelly dead animal in the dog's mouth. "Gross! Get away from me!" He started running and managed to kick what appeared to be a squirrel skull like a football, offering up his most successful sports move in all of his spectacularly non-athletic life. He was beginning to wonder if he were in the middle of a Twilight Zone episode, Twilight Zone being a scary show Ernest got to watch on TV. Carl's own parents, on the other hand, thought the show was too much for a kid. Plus it came on after his bedtime.

Carl was making so much noise his father came running through the trees, thinking something terrible had happened. When he saw the dog chasing after Carl with a poor dead possum hanging from his muzzle, Pops started laughing so hard the dog stopped and looked at him, dropping the possum as he tried to smile at the hollering boy and the laughing man.

Pops kicked the possum into the creek, which made the dog go chasing after it. Carl said, "Don't kick that dead thing into the creek, it's dirty enough without a dead body in it!"

His father answered, "That's not the first dead thing to be in that creek. There was a Civil War battle fought around here almost exactly 100 years ago. I bet there were a lot of dead bodies in the creek back then."

"Do you think they're still there, Pops?' Carl asked as a shiver ran up his spine.

Made in the USA
Charleston, SC
10 February 2012

He never seemed to get tired of fetching the stick, which became wetter and wetter with drool each time he brought it back.

But this time, instead of returning the stick to Carl after the first throw, he took it to the white kid across the way. The white kid looked at the stick, he looked at Possum, he smiled at Carl, and then he threw the stick.

Carl decided at that moment, what with Dr. King and the new Civil Rights Act, it was time for him to actually meet a white kid. After gathering up all the courage he had, he walked over to the boy and asked his name.

"Tommy," the boy answered.

"I'm Carl and this is Possum. He's a stray. I'm trying to talk my dad into letting me have him."

Tommy laughed and said, "He looks more like a wolf than a possum."

Carl said, "How he got his name is kind of a long story."

"I've got all day," Tommy responded. "I just moved here and don't know anybody." He pointed to one of the new houses Carl's father was helping to build, the only one that was finished so far."

"So, you are one of the rich kids who are gonna be living in this neighborhood."

"We aren't rich. That's for sure. My daddy just got a new job teaching at Georgia Tech and college teachers don't make much money."

"Well, you're gonna have a swimming pool, right?"

"Maybe a kiddie pool in the back yard. That's the only pool we can afford. My mother had to borrow money from my grandmother just got get us moved."

Carl looked at Tommy and thought that maybe he and this white boy could be friends after all. They sat down by the creek and talked. Carl told Tommy about his mother and his dad and his annoying little sister, and how he was supposed to be helping out at

the construction site. He also told him about his friend, Ernest, and how they wanted to be comic book writers when they grew up.

Tommy told Carl about his annoying little brother and his mother and father, and about his best friend, Donnie, back up in Ohio, where they'd just moved from. And Tommy told Carl that he, too, wanted to be a writer when he grew up.

Before long, Carl and Tommy were talking excitedly about meeting up the next day with pencils and paper so they could start work on the comic book they would write together, just the two of them, during that summer of 1964. Possum sat and watched them, his tongue hanging out, a smile on his face.

A few days later, as the boys sat on the sticky stump that used to be the big old oak tree, planning the plot of their comic book, Possum, for some strange reason, started digging.

CHAPTER 7

FRANCES
2010

The next afternoon, Frances and Clyde were down by the creek. Frances had a hammer and a screw driver and was attempting to pry the lid off the tin box. She'd already tried the keys from the Maxine keychain but there wasn't a lock on the box; it was just stuck.

After a lot of jamming the screwdriver into the small crevice between the box and the lid, and a good bit of hammering the end of the screwdriver, it looked like Frances was making some progress. By turning the box around and around and prying and hammering, the lid was becoming undone from the box. The good news was that Clyde had found what looked to be an ancient bone and he was busy gnawing on that instead of trying to help.

It was shady down by the creek, especially in the late afternoon, with the sun passing behind her house. Frances knew she didn't have much time. Her mother was going to want her to set the table, saying something like, "Frankie, dinner doesn't make itself!"

Finally! The top popped off. Frances was having a hard time seeing, but she knew there were several things inside. She'd certainly shaken it around enough to know that. She hoped she hadn't broken anything.

As the lid came off, Frances saw what looked to be several pieces of notebook paper attached together with brads. It appeared to be a kid-made comic book, written in pencil and colored with crayons, with boxes and drawings and words written in bubbles.

Just as she was trying to figure out the comic book, Frances heard her mother's voice calling.

"Tom, will you call Frankie up to supper?"

Frances knew she would still have a few minutes because her daddy would want to hit a few more golf balls before he made her come up to wash her hands. She was anxious to see what else was in the box, and wished the light was better. Maybe after supper, she could make up an excuse to come back down with a flashlight. As if her mother would let her do that.

Suddenly, "What on earth do you have there, Frankie?" It was her dad, golf club in hand, peering down at her.

Busted!

"I found it! I found it here by the creek! I was going to tell. I'm sorry!"

Frances' father looked at Frances and at the tin box and at the papers in her hand. He appeared puzzled and a bit strange.

"Jupiter Man," he finally said.

"What?"

"Jupiter Man."

"What?" Frances was confused. What was he talking

about?

"Jupiter Man. I haven't thought about Jupiter Man in

years." Her father sat down on the stump next to Frances. "Look at

what it says at the bottom of that first page."

Frances looked, pulling the paper close so she could read.

"It says 'Jupiter Man, written and illustrated by Carl and Tommy.'"

She looked at her father, so many questions in her head.

"Yep, that Tommy was your very own, good old dad."

"Really? You put the box here?" Frances was still confused,

with all sorts of questions bubbling up in her brain. "Why didn't

you ever tell me? Who was Carl? What else did you put in it?"

Just then, "Tom! Where's Frankie? I need you both here to

help me. Supper's almost ready."

Frances' father saw the look on her face that asked that they

not tell Mom just yet, so he said, "Can you hide the box until

tomorrow? Tomorrow we can talk about it and I'll tell you what I know."

Frances and her father walked up to the house, hand in hand, Clyde following behind them, the old but tasty bone still cracking in his teeth. Frances was pretty sure she wouldn't sleep that night as excited as she was. And she wasn't all that interested in sitting around the kitchen table eating dinner or talking about the weather either.

The next morning, bright and early, Frances, Clyde, and the grown-up Tommy were back down by the creek, sitting on the stump, and talking about the box. Frances' mother was busy with errands, so she hadn't even asked what their plans were for the day.

Dad got started with his explanation. "Remember me telling you about the summer my parents, your grandparents, bought this house? I was so homesick and I missed my best friend, Donnie, back up in Ohio. That was the summer they cut down this tree. It

was a big old beautiful tree and they just cut it down. All of this land had been part of an old estate. It was sold and then divided up into several different plots for smaller houses to be built on. I think the tree was just too big for those smaller yards."

"I remember you saying that you saw them cut it down."

"Yes, I did, and that's the day I met my first black friend. His name was Carl. He was hanging around helping out his dad who was a construction worker on some of the new houses that were being built. He had sort of adopted a stray dog he called Possum."

"What do you mean, your first black friend? I have lots of black friends and some brown ones too, like William Perez."

"Things were different then, Frances. We didn't go to school with kids of different colors. I didn't even know any black people. It's hard to believe that we now have a black president. So much history has happened in my lifetime."

Frances was getting a bit irritated. "So Carl was black and you were white and you became friends and wrote the comic book

and put it in a tin box in the woods down by the creek. Why did you do that and why didn't you come back and get it?" Frances then looked her father square in the eye and added, "And why didn't you tell me about it?"

"I didn't tell you because I forgot all about it. I know it's crazy, but it was a long time ago, and after that summer, I got to know a lot of new kids when school started and I got busy and I totally forgot about the tin box. And I never saw Carl or Possum again. I know it sounds crazy but it's true. Later I went off to college and then got a job. Finally, I met your mom and we got married and had you. We only moved back here a few years ago when I inherited this house from your grandparents. I'm sorry Pumpkin. I've just had a lot on my mind."

Frances felt sorry for her daddy, thinking about him losing his job and being so depressed, so she said, "That's okay. I forgive you." After a moment though, she continued with, "But I need to know more about the box. What else did you put in it?"

"We just put in the comic book. The other stuff was already in there. That crazy dog, Possum, dug it up. He dug up the box. Well, he started digging and then we helped him. We never told anybody about it. I can't remember exactly what was in it, although I do remember something that looked to have been from the Civil War. And I have no idea who put the rest of it in there. Carl and I figured it was some kind of time capsule. That's why we decided to put our comic book in, since it was so much a part of that summer. We buried it again, right here, right next to where we found it, right here next to the stump."

Frances' father stopped for a minute, scratching his head. "I do remember, when we found it, it was in a beat up old wooden box. Carl replaced the wooden box with the tin one. I think it was one his father used to keep nails. And we wrapped the whole thing in what Carl called a croker sack. It was a kind of burlap sack that things like potatoes came in."

Frances had heard enough. She was dying to see what was in the box. She got up from where she was sitting, and with Clyde's

help, she took the box from under the bush and brought it over to her father and opened it.

On top was the comic book. She already knew about that and who'd put it there, so she set it aside. Next she found what appeared to be a journal, a very old journal, wrapped in some kind of cloth. She looked in it, quickly noting the damaged pages and a few drawings. She decided she would come back to that later. Her father was quiet, letting her discover for herself without interrupting.

There were several other items. They seemed heavy. A couple were rolling around in the bottom of the box and Frances couldn't see what they were. She put her hand in and pulled out a flat stone, which didn't seem all that interesting, until she noticed the carvings.

Next was something made of wood.

When Frances lifted it out of the box, she saw that it looked like a big spool, something that once held thread or yarn. The spool

had been decorated to look like a bride, with a face drawn on. The white dress was made of lace, and a veil had been sewn to yarn hair. The bride was a little dirty, but Frances thought she was pretty.

One more thing in the bottom of the box. It was heavy and shaped like a cylinder.

When Frances pulled it out of the box, she saw that it was really old. She couldn't tell what it was. She held it out to her father.

"That's the one I remember, Frances, the one we thought was from the Civil War." He picked it up and investigated it thoroughly, as if looking for evidence of something mysterious and very important.

"It looks like an old bullet. I remember Carl mentioning his father had told him about the Battle of Peachtree Creek that was fought right around here, so maybe someone put the bullet in the box as a reminder of the battle."

That was it. All that was in the tin box. Frances shook it one last time to make sure. She had so many questions.

Frances and her father spent a long time together down by the creek that morning, looking at all the things that were in the box, wondering about who had put them there and why. In looking, her father remembered them all, and in remembering what was in the box, he remembered that summer with Carl and wondered what had ever happened to him.

Finally, Frances sat back and said, "Daddy, do we have to tell Mama about this? I'm afraid she'll want to call the police or something."

Frances' father said, "Yep, I think we should share this with your mother. I think you'll be surprised. You know, these past couple of years have been hard on our family. I believe it will be good for the three of us to have something special like this to share."

"But Mama won't approve of me pulling something out of the creek. She doesn't like for me to get dirty."

"Your mother just wants you to be safe and happy. Let's go see if she's home."

Frances dragged her feet all the way back up to the house, dreading what her mother was going to say and do. Her father had her wait on the patio while he went in to talk to her mother.

Frances was nervous, afraid her mama would be mad that she'd disobeyed her by playing down by the creek and keeping a secret. Clyde gave her a concerned look but immediately stretched out and went to sleep in the warm sun, snoring happily as his eyeballs danced under his fuzzy black lids.

Frances waited for what seemed to be a very long time, but when her parents came back outside, she was surprised by her mother's positive attitude and how excited she was to see what Frances had unearthed from Peachtree Creek. Her mother even seemed to understand that this was Frances' discovery and not

hers, and she didn't mention the notion of calling the newspaper or the police or the Atlanta History Center. Frances thought that must have been *some* talk her mama and daddy had had while she waited on the patio, listening to Clyde snore. Parents were certainly strange people.

"You do think we should re-bury it, right?" Frances' mom even asked, actually sitting on the stump down by the creek, not looking for hobos *or* snakes. "What are you going to add to the box?"

Frances suddenly had an idea of something she and her parents could do together, something that might help her and her father and her mother understand each other better and quit being mad and depressed.

"You know, since we don't know why all these things were put in the box or who put them there, maybe we could make up stories about the people. And write them down."

Frances' father thought for a minute and then looked more excited than he had in months. "You mean we could write a fictional account of kids who might have put these things here and why? Maybe write a book? Something that would help other kids learn about the history of Atlanta?"

Frances added, "Along with William Perez's help. He's a really good writer."

After just a moment's hesitation, and a look from her father to her mother, both of her parents said, "Of course!"

Frances was happy. It looked like she and her dad would be spending more time together and maybe her mother too. And perhaps she'd learn something about the people who'd lived before her right where she was living now, the history of her home town. It was something to think of all the stories those people could tell, and even their secrets. Maybe that's why they put those things in the box, to share their secrets in some way.

After a few minutes with everyone lost in thought, Frances said, "I think I've even got a name for the book."

"What?" asked her parents.

"Secret Stories from Peachtree Creek."

"Perfect!" her mom and dad said.

Clyde just sat and smiled, slobber running down his chin and onto his big black paws. For some strange reason, he was thinking about digging a hole over by the old tree stump.

CHAPTER 8

A GROWN-UP'S GUIDE TO
SECRET STORIES FROM PEACHTREE CREEK

The idea for *Secret Stories from Peachtree Creek* grew from my frustration with trying to teach Georgia History to my second graders in a manner that made sense to them and in a way that was interesting. These particular children were lucky to live in an area steeped in so much history, but they still thought it all not only happened long ago but also far away. I needed a way to capture their attention and "prove" it had transpired right where they live now.

The idea came to me when we were on a field trip to the Atlanta History Center. The guide was telling us about the Battle of Peachtree Creek, and several of my students said that Peachtree Creek ran behind their houses. As someone new to Atlanta, I was struck by that fact that history had occurred right where the children lived. As someone who grew up in Savannah, that should have been old news to me, but I'm a slow learner.

And so, I wrote the stories. I wrote them primarily for the history they provide and not for any great literary value, but I hope they are interesting enough to help start some discussions in classrooms or around the dinner table. Although children can certainly read the stories themselves, they were designed to be used as read-alouds. Because my time was limited, I read each story in one sitting, which was most likely too long. If I had had more freedom and time, I would have read each story in two or three sittings with discussions interspersed.

Below are some themes, discussion items, and research topics I hope will be helpful.

Themes

The theme of place was what first brought me to writing the stories; the notion that history happened right where we are, not just some place far away.

The theme of time is also important to the stories, how time affects most things without changing big ideas like love, compassion, family, fairness, acceptance, learning, survival and humor.

The changes that occurred included the pollution in the creek, urban renewal with the estate being transformed into smaller plots of land while trees are cut down, how people become educated, how natural things grow and age (the oak tre

I used some commonalities to help children understand the place was the same and some things don't change. The black dogs, bird's nests, dead possums, and squirrel skulls, while perhaps a bit far-fetched, were included to force that idea. In addition, I used references to other stories to make further connections. Susannah thought a red fox had come up behind her, a black bear for Rosie.

Suggested Discussion Topics per Chapter

Chapter 1 Frances

1. Have your parents ever wanted you to be different than you are? Do they sometimes want you to do things you don't want to do? If so, what? Why do you think they do this?
2. Has something bad or difficult ever happened to your family? If so, what was it and how did your family handle it?
3. Have you ever kept a secret from your mother or father? Why did you keep this secret and how did you feel about it?
4. Is it ever okay to keep a secret from your parents? If so, what and why?
5. Have you ever noticed that your mother or father was sad? If so, what did you do?

Chapter 2 Tuck

1. What were the clues that Tuck was Native American?
2. What clues helped you to suspect that Tuck may have lived in the same place as Frances?
3. How was Tuck's life different from Frances' life? How was it the same?
4. Have you ever been bullied? If so, what did you do about it?

5. Do you sometimes make up stories in your head? Why do you think people do that?

Chapter 3 Susannah

1. Have you ever moved to a new place? If so, how did it feel? Were you excited or sad? How long did it take you to get used to your new home?
2. Have you ever had a friend you knew your parents wouldn't like? If so, what did you do about it?
3. Susannah had a job in her father's store. What do your parents expect you to do to help out?
4. Susannah thought her father was wrong not to like the Indians who lived near them. Do you think your parents are sometimes wrong? If so, how and when?
5. What do you think happened to Senoya when her family left?

Chapter 4 James

1. Can you imagine what it was like to belong to someone other than your parents? What do you think James' life was like on the plantation? What would it be like not to be able to read or write?
2. It's difficult to imagine that people used to walk long distances. What do you think it was like to walk barefooted for miles and miles and then to sleep outside without a sleeping bag or a tent?
3. How was the Civil War different from the wars we have now? How was it the same?
4. Would your parents ever put you "in harm's way"? If so, what would be the circumstances?
5. Why is James' story so much a part of the mystery in the book

Chapter 5 Rosie

1. Even though she was only ten years old, Rosie had to work long hours. Why do you think that happened and was it fair? Are there young children today who have to work instead of going to school? If so, where and why?
2. Rosie moved from a very small home to a very large one, but she wasn't happy. What makes a home a happy one?
3. Rosie named the dogs after members of her family. If you have a pet, what did you name him or her? Where did the name come from?
4. Rosie was wrong about the rich people who lived in the big old house. Have you ever been wrong about someone, and, if so, what made you change your mind?
5. How did finding the mama dog and her puppies cause Rosie's health to improve?

Chapter 6 Carl

1. How was it that Carl had never met a white person?
2. Carl wanted to be a comic book writer when he grew up. What do you want to be and why?
3. What do you think gave Carl the courage to walk over to meet Tommy?
4. Why do you think Carl was sad to see the big old tree cut down?
5. Do you think Carl and Tommy would have ever become friends if the circumstances had been different?

Chapter 7 Frances

1. Frances had several surprises in this chapter. What were they?

2. Frances was mad at her father when she first found out he had known about the box. Why do you think she was so mad?
3. Why didn't Frances want her father to tell her mother about her discovery?
4. Why was that last item at the bottom of the box so important to the mystery?
5. How did finding the box help to make Frances' relationship with her parents better? How might her discovery help her entire family?

General Discussion Topics

1. What changed in the book and what stayed the same?
2. How were the children's lives the same and how were they different?
3. When did you figure out that all the children lived in the same place? What clues were available to help you with that?
4. Which character was your favorite and why?
5. What do you think the characters did when they grew up? Do you think any of them went back to the oak tree by Peachtree Creek and tried to dig up what was buried there?
6. If you were to bury something in the box by Peachtree Creek, what would it be?
7. Could this story have happened some place else other than Peachtree Creek? Why or why not?
8. Peachtree Creek is still quite polluted. What can you do to make it cleaner? Why should it matter if it's clean or not?
9. Should Frances and her family have told others about the box for "the sake of history"? If so, why?
10. Why is it important to study history and to learn about geography?

Topics for Further Research

1. The Chattahoochee River and Peachtree Creek
2. The Civil War
3. Child Labor
4. Creek and Cherokee Indians
5. The Cherokee Alphabet
6. The Trail of Tears
7. Martin Luther King Jr and the Civil Rights Movement
8. The history of Atlanta and Buckhead (or any other home town)
9. Personal Family History
10. The History of Dogs

ABOUT THE AUTHOR

Marcia Mayo has taught all ages from three-year-olds to graduate students. She didn't know she enjoyed history until she'd lived long enough to realize it was happening during her lifetime and at her own back door. Marcia enjoys helping children see the connections between history and their own lives.

Marcia lives in Atlanta, Georgia in a building where Margaret Mitchell once lived and she spends her summers in Portland, Oregon, very near to where Lewis, Clarke, and Sacagawea happened upon the Pacific Ocean.